The Princess and the Pea

Based on a story by
Hans Christian Andersen

Retold by Matthew Oldham

Illustrated by Lorena Alvarez

Reading consultant: Alison Kelly

There was once a young
prince who loved going
on adventures.

He was good at finding treasure.

He was very good at
rescuing people...

...and he was very, very
good at fighting dragons.

But when the prince came
back home, he felt sad.

"I wish I had someone to
share my adventures with,"
he said to himself.

One day, he had an idea...

"I will find someone to
marry!" he cried.

He asked his parents for help. They were the king and queen, after all.

I want to get married!

His parents were delighted.
"We'll help you find the perfect
princess," said the king.

At last!

The king and queen
wrote to every princess
in the world. Royal
servants set off
to deliver the
invitations.

PRINCESS
WANTED

Dozens of princesses came to
the palace to meet the prince.
Some came with lots of servants.

10

Some came dripping
with diamonds.

One even came riding
an elephant.

The prince tried to tell them about his adventures, but they were only interested in his treasure.

"They don't seem like *real* princesses to me," he sighed. "Real princesses should want excitement and adventure."

The king and queen
called their best inventors
to a meeting.

"We need a test," the
queen demanded, "to find
a real princess."

The inventors tried all sorts of different tests, but none of their ideas worked.

Then, one inventor said...

"I know how to find
a real princess!"

The prince stepped forward.
"How?" he asked.

Two servants pulled back an enormous sheet to reveal a very unusual bed... with a *tower* of mattresses.

"This is the finishing touch,"
said the inventor. She put a
dried pea in the prince's hand.

"How will this help?" asked the prince, giving back the pea.

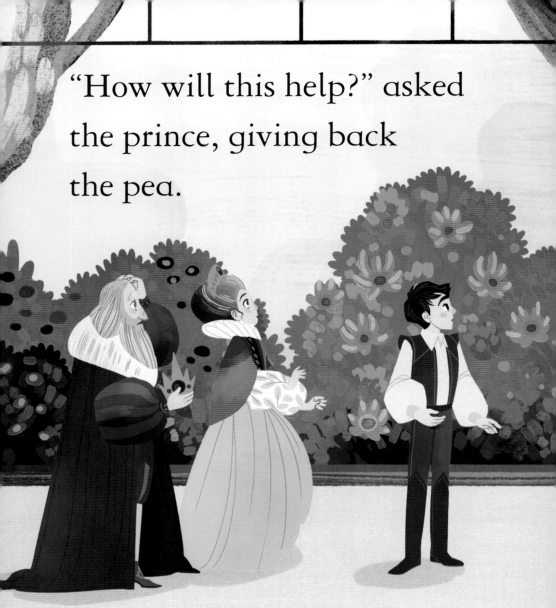

"A real princess notices everything around her," explained the inventor.

"She will be able to feel
this pea through all
these mattresses."

The prince invited more
princesses to the palace...

...but none of them
passed his test.

In the morning, each of them declared, "What a comfortable bed!"

Mmm, such a lovely sleep.

The prince felt sad again.

After a while, the princesses
stopped coming. The prince
seemed too hard to please.

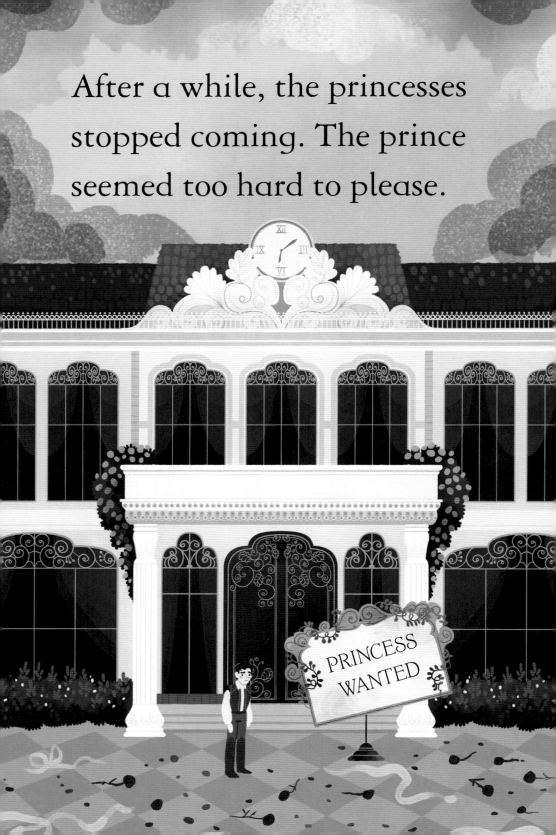

PRINCESS WANTED

The prince gave up hope, too.
He thought he'd never find
someone to marry.

Then, late one night...

KABOOM! Thunder crashed. Lightning flashed. Rain fell in big, fat drops.

Through the noise of the storm, the prince heard a thump on the door.

A wet, shivering girl stood on the palace doorstep.

"I was caught in the storm," said the girl. "May I shelter here tonight?"

The girl's sweet voice charmed the prince. He didn't notice her tangled hair or muddy clothes.

"You may stay for as long as you like," said the prince.

Squelch   Squelch

As the girl warmed up, the prince told her all about his adventures.

The girl listened to every word.

All this talking made the
prince feel sleepy.

Soon, he couldn't keep his
eyes open.

When the prince woke up, he was alone. The girl had gone.

The next morning, the
prince stared gloomily
at his breakfast.

"Why not go on another
adventure?" asked the queen.
"That will cheer you up."

The prince sighed. He didn't want to go on another adventure all alone.

Just then, the girl walked in.

The prince jumped up.
"Where have you been?"
he asked.

"After you fell asleep, I looked for a bed," she replied.

"The one I found was very tall. I had to climb in using a ladder."

"Oh?" said the prince, surprised. "How... how did you sleep?"

"Not very well," answered the girl. "I think you need a new bed. That one has a hard lump in the middle."

The king threw up
his hands.

The queen fell
off her chair.

Ohhh!

The prince's face turned pale,
as he stared at the girl.

"You're a real princess!"
he gasped.

Now the princess looked surprised too. "How did you know?" she asked.

When the prince told her about the pea, the princess started to giggle.

"I've been looking for a real
PRINCE!" she said.

"I've journeyed from palace to palace, looking for a brave prince," the princess explained.

"Everyone has turned me away... except you."

The real prince married the real princess the very next day.

The prince and princess never stopped having adventures. They built a museum for all the treasure they found.

In the middle, they put the
pea in a beautiful crystal case.

It may still be there today.

About the story

The Princess and the Pea was written by Hans Christian Andersen in 1835. He was born in Denmark in 1805. He left home at fourteen to seek his fortune and became famous all over the world as a writer of fairy tales.

Designed by Laura Nelson and Sam Whibley
Series Designer: Russell Punter
Edited by Rob Lloyd Jones
Series editor: Lesley Sims

This edition first published in 2018 by Usborne Publishing Ltd., Usborne House, 83-85 Saffron Hill, London EC1N 8RT, England. www.usborne.com